Let's Change That!

If Animals Can, We Can, Too!

FERNE PRESS

Written by Dr. Bashar Salame and Illustrated by Rainer M. Osinger

Let's Change That! If Animals Can, We Can, Too!

Copyright © 2014 by Bashar Salame

Layout and cover design by Jacqueline L. Challiss Hill
Illustrations created by Rainer M. Osinger
Illustrations created with highly pigmented artist watercolor

Printed in the United States of America

Summary: When Felix is presented with a situation, he decides to change his thinking to fix the problem.

Library of Congress Cataloging-in-Publication Data
Salame, Bashar
Let's Change That!/Bashar Salame–First Edition
ISBN-13: 978-1-938326-34-9
1. Perception. 2. Working together. 3. Getting along. 4. Believing in oneself.
5. Relationships. 6. Confidence.
I. Salame, Bashar II. Title
Library of Congress Control Number: 2014938634

FERNE PRESS

Ferne Press is an imprint of Nelson Publishing & Marketing
366 Welch Road, Northville, MI 48167
www.nelsonpublishingandmarketing.com
(248) 735-0418

Dedicated to Jude, Amelie, and everyone who's ever tried to break stereotypes and change the world. I'm blessed, humbled, and honored by the support and love of my wife, Sueha, my parents, my family, and my friends who constantly encourage and motivate me to be a better man, father, and global citizen. I hope you enjoy reading this story and it sparks the positive change advocated by all.

"Felix!" shouted his owner.
"DON'T GO OUTSIDE!"
But it was too late.

"Tricked you again," Felix laughed,
as he raced into the backyard
to see what he could find.

Felix found a bird who was struggling on the ground.

"Little bird, why are you not flying away?"

The little bird was just jumping,
but his wings didn't flap long
or hard enough to make him fly.

"Oh, my baby!" Felix heard.

"Who said that?" asked Felix.
It didn't come from the small bird
but from a large tree
where Mama Bird stood
near her nest.

"My baby has fallen from our nest! And now there's a cat!" Mama Bird chirped, as she flapped her wings.

"I need to do something, but what?" Felix realized.

Just then Felix saw his friend Omar running across the street.
"Omar!" Felix shouted, as he ran toward his friend.

"Felix," said Omar, "what are you doing outside? You're an indoor cat."

"It's a good thing I'm out.
There's a baby bird that needs our help," replied Felix.

"What? Are you serious? We don't help birds; we chase them,"
Omar said plainly.

"Let's change that!" answered Felix. "Maybe Bonnie can help us!"

"Oh man, you've been inside way too long. Are you kidding me?
Bonnie is a dog and dogs chase cats.
Everyone knows that," answered Omar.

"If I can control myself and not chase this bird,
maybe I can convince Bonnie
not to chase me and we can work together," Felix replied.

Felix knew Bonnie would be near her favorite fire hydrant, so he ran in that direction.

"It's going to be a mess of whiskers, feathers, and fur. We're all doomed!"

Omar panicked and took cover.

Bonnie was walking
near her hydrant.
She saw Felix, smiled, and ran toward him.
Bonnie stopped a few steps from Felix.
Felix did not run; he just stood there.

"What are you up to?" Bonnie asked.
"I don't trust cats;
they can be sneaky."

"A baby bird fell from our tree,
and I want to return
him to his home.
Mama Bird is worried,"
Felix replied.

"I have a plan,
but Mama Bird needs to trust us.
And if we can be friends, maybe she
doesn't have to be afraid of us."

"Now that would truly be something,"
Bonnie responded.

Bonnie and Felix walked
to the large tree together.
"There he is," Felix told Bonnie.
The baby bird was closer to the tree
but still unable to return to his nest.

"Oh no, the cat's back," Mama Bird chirped.

"Mama Bird, I know this sounds strange,
but we want to help your baby," Bonnie shouted.

"A cat and dog want to help a bird?
That's not how things work,"
said Mama Bird.

Bonnie simply replied,
"Let's change that!"

Bonnie told Mama Bird the plan.
"Dogs can't climb trees, but cats can.
Felix is going to let Baby Bird grab onto his fur
and he's going to climb this tree.
When he's done, since cats don't climb down trees that well,
I'm going to catch him when he jumps."

Mama smiled as much as a bird could.
"Okay, Baby Bird,
I need you to stay calm and let these guys help us."

"I can't believe they're going to try this,"
Omar said nervously.

Baby Bird grabbed onto Felix and
even though it hurt a little, Felix didn't mind.
"Hold on tight, Baby."
He climbed up the tree like only a cat can.

"That was amazing!
Thank you, thank you!"
Mama Bird said with joy.

"You're welcome!"

"I hope this works,"
Felix said nervously as he jumped toward Bonnie.
She caught Felix like a toy.
Bonnie didn't hurt him at all and gently set him down.

Omar shouted,
"Did that just happen? Awesome!"

Bonnie looked at Felix. "That was brave. I'll never look at cats the same."

"Wow! We worked together," Felix responded.
"Cats can help birds and dogs can help cats. It starts by saying,

'LET'S CHANGE THAT!'"

Dr. Bashar Salame has been a practicing chiropractor in the metro Detroit area for over ten years. He currently owns and operates two clinics, focusing on enhancing the health and well-being of others. He is a married father of a four-year-old boy named Jude and a two-year-old girl named Amelie. Among the family's most cherished activities is reading stories and exploring books together. Their favorite authors include Dr. Seuss, Mo Willems, Greg Foley, Shel Silverstein, and Ferne Press's own Carol McCloud. For more information, please visit basharsalame.com.

Rainer M. Osinger is an illustrator, graphic designer, painter, and children's book author. He studied graphics and illustration at (NDC) New Design University in St. Pölten, Austria. He is married and a proud father of seven wonderful children. Rainer lives with his family in St.Veit/Glan Kärnten, Austria. For more information about Rainer and his work, please visit www.osinger-grafik.at.